Nightshade
The devils inn

Introduction

Would you sell your soul for love? If it meant you could spend eternity with that person, even if it was in hell, would it be worth it? My name is Christian Hail, and recently I've been contemplating exactly what I'm willing to do for love. I could say it started with a girl, but in reality I was damned long before she walked into my life, I guess my fate was sealed when I was a kid, abandoned at birth I bounced around from group home to group home in Waltzburg City, it wasn't long before I was in a juvenile detention center, from there on I was in and out of jail and prison until my recent release a few months ago. My parole officer got me a job as a maintenance man at a motel, the pay was crap but the job came with a free room, and with no other place to live it was the Nightshade Motel or prison, thinking back now, I should have chose prison. In the end I would be given a choice, to kill the woman I loved in order to save her, or kill myself to be with her.

Episode 1

Looking to get wet?

"Looking to get wet?" those were the first words she spoke to me, this woman who would change my life forever. My day started off just like the days before, wake up, make a cup of coffee, head over to the Motel managers office, listen to him tell me about his pregnant wife and how much he's looking forward to being a dad, get a list from him of all the repairs that need to be made around the motel, and then start my day of slavery. This particular day started off with me cleaning the pool, and thats when I heard her voice, while crouched down staring into an algae filled pool, when I turned to look behind me towards the sound of her voice, I quickly was struck by her beauty, the only way to describe her, is that she looked like sin,

standing there
wearing mini shorts,
G-string showing with
a bikini top, her body
curved in angles
design to illicit a
singular response in
men, I knew her type,
criminals are like
scavengers, we feed
off the weak and sick
and thrive off death,
trust me, I have done
my fare share of

crimes to know, from selling drugs to single mothers, to robbing hard working fathers at gun point, there was a time I was the worst of them, so when I saw her I knew she was trouble. I had made up my mind before I got out of prison that I wasn't going to go back, I had already given prison to much of my life already, now at 34 years old, I was done with the streets, but hell, I'm a guy, so I had to talk to her. She said her name was Cherry, and then jokingly asked again if I wanted to get wet, boy did I want to get wet, and she knew it, her eyes stared through me, straight to the animal within that she could tame with a whisper, her seduction was primal, however skills like hers weren't earned through mundane experiences, she was a pro, and her touch cost more than I could pay.

Cherry; "So how long you been out?"

Christian Hail;
"You could tell that
easy?"

Cherry; "Yeah it's
kinda obvious, prison
tats, working a dead
end job at a rundown
motel, I mean this
couldn't have been
your dream job, so
when did you get
out?"

Christian Hail; "A few months ago"

Cherry; "I've been here awhile yet this is the first time I've seen you, so where were you before you ended up here?"

Christian Hail; "I was in a half way house before a few weeks ago when I started working here, but I'm sure you already know exactly when I started this job considering your the neighborhood watch"

Cherry; "What can I say, I just like to know whats going on within my surroundings"

Christian Hail; "I feel you, knowledge is power"

Cherry; "So when are you looking to go back to prison?"

Christian Hail;
"Never, I'm done
with the streets"

Cherry; "Well that
might become a
problem if we're
going to be friends"

Christian Hail;
"Who said we were
going to be friends?"

Cherry; "I just have a feeling"

She intrigued me to say the least, but what did she want from me? That question would be answered sooner than I thought. A few minutes into our conversation she received a phone call, her cell phone ring tone caught me off guard, it was a nursery rhyme from a children's book called "Cherry at the tree top" it was weird, I remembered reading that book all the time when I was a little kid, "Cherry Chime crawled up the tree, she fell back down and bumped her knee, Cherry Chime

wanted a leaf, but
could not climb the
tree, Cherry Chime
got on her feet, but
refused to turn and
leave, Cherry chime
began to climb, then
whoops she fell asleep,
Cherry Chime woke
up that night and all
the leaves were gone,
but Cherry Chime
didn't fear cause
they'll be back at

dawn, Cherry Chime tried everyday for as long as the day is long, and Cherry Chime finally got her leaf when she grew big and strong" I remembered thinking as a kid that Cherry Chime was such and idiot, who would work that hard to get a leaf, I mean couldn't you just get one off the ground? I never did ever figure out the meaning to that story, but I had a feeling that in some twisted way, by being around this mysterious girl, I would figure it out, or at least figure out her understanding. When she got off the phone I had to ask her about her name.

Christian Hail;
"Cherry Chime?"

Cherry; "Huh?"

Christian Hail;
"Your name, did you
get it from that
book?"

Cherry; "Honestly, I don't even remember, a lot of my past is a blank, but I remember this nursery rhyme of all things, as for my name, I think its always been Cherry"

How does someone not know their own name? I couldn't help

but think she was
pulling my leg, but
she seemed serious,
was she and orphan
like me? Is that why
she didn't know what
her real name was? As
a kid I would wonder
what my name was,
my real name that my
parents gave me
before they gave me
away. After and
awkward silence she

told me she had to go get ready because she had a friend coming over, and like that, she was gone, and I was back to my mundane existence. After cleaning the pool and doing a few other repairs, I decided to turn in for the day. Oodles of noodles, a glass of tap water and shit tv, the highlight of my day, a world in chaos, war, death, famine, and yet every channel theres something about The West End Boyz, Jesus Christ, whats peoples obsession with these mediocre boy bands, I've been bored before but this was different, I knew this feeling, this itch that I needed to scratch that

would drive me crazy
until I scratched it, I
wanted to get into
trouble, I needed to
fight someone or
worse, I needed sex,
money, drugs,
alcohol, I needed to
be me, the person I
was trying so hard not
to be, these thoughts
began to overwhelm
me, I couldn't handle
being broke, feeling

weak and powerless, cleaning up after other people like a slave, these feelings weren't new, at least once or twice a week I would have my weekly mental breakdowns, after a shower and sleep I would usually go back to my right mind, but this day was different, before I could calm down, I heard a scream, when I walked outside of my room I could hear where the screams were coming from and rushed towards them, once I reached the room I tried banging on the door calling in to whoever was inside, yet the screaming didn't stop, it sounded as if a woman was being attacked, there wasn't anytime to call the police or get help, it was up to me to help whoever was inside. What was going on in room 33? I couldn't hesitate, I kicked in the door and quickly rushed in, Cherry was curled up in the corner crying and there was a guy by her bed trying to get dressed, my mind pieced everything together before I could even process it, instinct kicked in and rage took over, within seconds I was on him, it had been so long since I could be the violent animal I was raised to be, the feeling of his flesh ripping beneath my fists, the sound of his bones cracking as he gurgled his blood, I would have beat him to death, until her phone rang, that fucking nursery rhyme again, when the rage passed I looked down and saw what I had done, the first thing I thought is he was gonna die and I would end up back in prison for the rest of my life. Covered in blood I turned to look at Cherry to see if she was ok, and with a sinister smile on her face she said, "See, I knew you wanted to get wet" in that moment I knew this girl was crazy, I didn't even know whether this guy had done anything wrong, I ran back to my room and shut the door, panic mode kicked in, I didn't know whether to run or call the cops and explain the situation, I started to pack what little belongings I had but before I could go anywhere I could hear the sirens, somehow the police had gotten to the motel within minutes, was this a setup? Did she call ahead of time and predict what I would do? Maybe someone heard her screams and called? These thoughts raced through my head, all I could do was sit on the floor and await my fate. Minutes turned to hours, and no cops came to arrest me, then out of nowhere, a knock on my door, when I got up to open it, I was sure it would be a cop, but instead, it was Cherry.

Cherry; "Hey"

Christian Hail; "Hey? I don't want anything to do with you"

Cherry; "Are you sure about that?"

Christian Hail; "I could have ended up back in prison cause of you"

Cherry; "What do you mean? You saved me"

Christian Hail;
"Saved you from
what? Tell me, what
did he do?"

Cherry; "Honestly,
nothing at all"

Christian Hail; "I
figured as much,
you're a psychopath,
do you get off on
crying rape?"

Cherry; "Rape? I never said a word, what, did you think he raped me? Awe, I didn't know you cared so much"

Christian Hail; "Look, I don't know what you're into, I just know I don't want to be apart of it"

Cherry; "We'll see, sooner or later, most likely sooner than later"

As she walked away, a sense of fear came over me, I've been through a lot of shit, and came across my fare share of gangsters, but this girl sent a chill down my spine that I couldn't explain. What was it about this girl? Why couldn't I just get her out my head? I had to get cleaned up, I was covered in blood but mainly I just needed a shower to clear my head, all I could see in my mind was her smile, she looked so pleased with herself, sitting there, watching me beat a guy to within an inch of his life, I felt played, but I must admit, I liked it. After my shower I needed to see her again so went to her room, 33, its the little coincidences for me, when I knocked the door crept open, I don't know why I continued or maybe I do, but I pushed open the door and thats when shit got real. Her room was illuminated by candles that shed light on a horrific scene born in the darkest of nightmares, the carpet was soaked in blood, so much it seemed to be overflowing, the walls of her room were covered in symbols painted in blood and feces, the smell was the worst part, it was indescribable, something I never smelled before, it nearly buckled me, it was as if the scent had weight to it and I could barely hold it, in the middle of the room was a bed, and on it was what was left of the guy I fought earlier, his body was dismembered and posed like a form of sick art, but where was Cherry? A part of me wanted to run, but something pulled me in, something in my needed to find her. When I entered the room, I could feel the blood gushing up from the carpet, I had

seen a lot in my life
yet nothing like this,
my body was shaking,
I was disgusted and
holding back the urge
to vomit, I made my
way to the bathroom,
the door was cracked
and I could see there
was candle light
coming from inside, I
slowly opened the
door as if that would
make what I was

going to find less crazy, when the door opened there she was, in a tub full of blood, before I could say a word she asked me once again.

Cherry; "Wanna get wet?"

For some reason I could feel tears swelling up in my

eyes, I wasn't sad, I just could feel I had made a mistake, a feeling of dread, like I was trapped now, as I turned to leave the front door slammed shut and the candles in the room blew out only leaving light coming from the candles in the bathroom, as I backed into the bathroom trying to figure out what was going on I shut and locked the bathroom door.

Cherry; "Whats wrong? You're not afraid are you?"

Christian Hail; "What the hell is going on here?"

Cherry; "Isn't it obvious? Its a party"

Christian Hail; "A party for what? What's out there?"

Cherry; "Who knows whats out there, as for this party, its yours silly"

Christian Hail; "A party for me? Why exactly?"

Cherry; "Its a rebirth day party, after tonight you'll be a whole new person"

She was confusing, every word she said was said in a nonchalant tone, but she seemed serious. Sounds began to start coming from outside

the bathroom,
something was
moving around the
room, heavy
breathing like some
sort of animal, what
ever it was it let out a
terrifying and strange
growl, it sounded like
a mix between a goat
and a lion, loud
enough to let me
know I should stay in
the bathroom, but low

enough that I didn't know if anyone outside the room heard it, I didn't know what to do, should I have screamed for help?

Christian Hail;
"What do you want
from me?"

Cherry; "I just want
you to live, the
question is what do
you want from me?
Whats it going to take

for you to live for
me?'"

Christian Hail; "I
guess I want to get
wet"

The candles blew
out, only for a second
but it was all she
needed, the candles
reignited and she was
standing in front of
me, naked, covered in

blood, she looked sexy as hell, I started to feel cold for some reason, I looked down and saw her hand plunged into my chest, in that moment I knew I was dead.

Cherry; "Wake up Mr Hail"

Christian Hail; "Mr Hail?"

Cherry; "Yeah, its not like you can be a christian anymore"

When I opened my eyes I was in bed, the room was normal again, no blood, no nothing, I felt relieved, was it just a dream? When I sat up there was a black goat with red eyes standing at the foot of the bed.

Mr Hail; "So then, shit happened?"

Cherry; "Yeah, shit happened"

To be continued…

www.ingramcontent.com/pod-product-compliance
Lightning Source LLC
Chambersburg PA
CBHW051527050726
47503CB00014B/2195